This Land

Barbadian short stories

Dorothy Lovell

Stories compiled and edited by Barbara Ann Chase

With love –
Nyah Bookclub
xx
June 2020

Chase Publications Church Hill Ch. Ch. Barbados.

Chase Publications.
Church Hill
Christ Church Barbados. Bb17070
barbarachase1439@gmail.com
www.barbaliciouscreative.com

Publisher's Note: This is a work of fiction. Names, characters, places, and incidents are a product of the author's imagination. Locales and public names are sometimes used for atmospheric purposes. Any resemblance to actual people, living or dead, or to businesses, companies, events, institutions, or locales is completely coincidental.

Compiled and edited by Barbara Ann Chase with Michelle Daniel

Book Layout © 2016 BookDesignTemplates.com

Cover photograph by Dr. Raymond Maughan
e-mail : raymond.maughan@gmail.com

Other photo credits – pages 46 & 71, supplied by the editor; page 66, compliments Shelley Clarke

Cover design by Michael Russell
e-mail : michael@aries83.com

Barbadian Short Stories/ Dorothy Lovell. – 1st ed.2019
Print Edition ISBN **978-976-8265-81-4**
Kindle Edition ISBN **978-976-8265-82-1**

Acknowledgements

Thanks to Starcom Network Inc.; and especially to
Charmaine Burns and to the Estate of Alfred Pragnell.

Also

to John Wickham for believing in
Dorothy's talent enough to showcase it to the world

Dedication

To all the old shop-keepers with pencils behind their ears and to those Barbadians who diligently tilled the soil- This land is ours

and

to John Lovell, who always encouraged and supported

She openeth her mouth with wisdom; and
her tongue is the law of kindness
Proverbs 31 verse 26

Contents

FOREWORD

The title of Dorothy Lovell's book of short stories, *This Land is Mine,* cannot help but recall for me the title of another series of artistic works also done about Barbados, *This is Not My Island.* The latter is a visual arts and video series by Nick Whittle, a British born Barbadian who made this country his home as an adult. Dorothy is, as we say in Bajan, a *bred and born Babajan,* but both may be claiming the same desire about this land that surely belongs to tourist, expatriate, adoptee, economic refugee and all de rest of we who find its perfumes sweet. From its colonial history it is said that the British parliamentary debates about the British settlement of Barbados, records one parliamentarian's remark that the island "is a marvelous piece of real estate". Dorothy Lovell's stories record it as more than that, and perhaps as a lost memory to her 1960s artistic sensibility.

The stories of *This Land is Mine* engender in all *ones* a desire for a Barbados that perhaps never existed. I mean, could an old man, grizzly and mean looking, fall so deeply in love with a baby that he could open his home and (perhaps) heart to a young destitute couple and their young children, when the last rung breaks off on their precarious ladder of life? Or could a young white plantation daughter, reminiscent of George Lamming's Amanda in his iconic novel, *In the*

Castle of My Skin fall in love with a black man? And that he could kill himself for love of her? Indeed, this story ends with her on the edge of the cliff from which he has jumped, and we are left sick at heart that she too will jump in classic Romeo and Juliette ill-fated style. Are these stories really believable? They are, and in being so enter the love song that some ill-advisably claim is missing from West Indian literature.

Somehow we all in this grey 21st century remember a gentler, a more caring, a more village Barbados. Dorothy Lovell's stories bring us sensuously there. Note in the lines below the careful recording of family connection that used to be done in a forgotten Barbados:

> He, Reuben had had no parents. His mother had died when he was a baby and his father had never taken any real interest in him. His cousin, Roy's father, uncle Doug, his mother's brother, was the only father he'd known…

The author is now within the lost world of Alzheimer's, and her daughter has chosen to honour with this record. But this is more than the sentimental play for sympathy it sounds. The eponymous story I am told has been read every Independence Day since the days of diffused radio Barbadians know as Rediffusion. Respected and literary Barbadian household names, Alfred Pragnell and Frank Collymore (the latter whose name is given to the premium national literary award) have provided the voices which bring alive Dorothy Lovell's characters and conditions in some of these stories. The celebrated *BIM magazine* (now *BIM Arts for the 21st Century*) published three of these stories, "The Shoe",

"Grannie's Birthday" and "Father Bear." This was under the magazine's second editor, veteran writer and newspaper man, John Wickham in the late 1960s and early 1970s. Recall, the first editor of *BIM* was acclaimed doyen of the arts in Barbados, Frank Collymore, and the earlier *BIM* had launched the careers of Caribbean great men of letters, Derek Walcott Nobel winner, George Lamming of *Castle* fame, and internationally acclaimed and much awarded poet Kamau Brathwaite.

The stories of *This Land is Mine* then is an independence gift by Dorothy Lovell to a land she both loves and writes very evocatively about. This book of stories is a daughter's wish not to let memory of her mother die.

I could write, as I had planned, very academically and convincingly about Dorothy Lovell's capacity to render the *livity* of the characters whom George Lamming calls "the people down below". I could advise students and writers wanting a taste of Barbadian relationships, before ZR public service vehicles made bus rides a pornographic adventure, about researching Dorothy Lovell's adventures in neighbourliness. I could even suggest with conviction that Dorothy Lovell in these stories provide linguistic voyages to satisfy any quest after one stream of the Bajan voice that shares literary provenance with Jeanette Lane-Clarke: (An example I cannot resist: "Who that out there? You gwine lick down de place?") DL shares some of JLCs bite, and far more of her loveliness in sentiment. I will do none of that.

Simply, I will do as Barbara (Lovell) Chase, Dorothy's daughter, my son's aunt and PJ the calypsonian's sister has done by presenting this collection, I will let Dorothy Lovell's words speak to you, dear reader.

Margaret D. Gill. PhD. Lits. in English
Carringtong1ll@yahoo.com

2019-09-28

ONE

GRANNIE'S BIRTHDAY

She sat in the old rocking chair that was so much out of keeping with the other furniture in the room, for the chair was almost as old as she was. Grannie was ninety years old today. As her old eyes gazed out upon a modern world, memories of an older and bygone era crowded her mind. She was never a person to sit and dream, but this morning as her children and grandchildren had sung 'Happy Birthday', it had brought back memories of her six little ones chanting the same refrain long, long ago, but in very different circumstances.

A fresh young voice recalled her to the present. "Grannie, where are you? Oh, there you are." This was Esther, her youngest son's daughter. That son and his family lived only a short distance from the daughter with whom Grannie now spent her days. Esther came and kissed her. "Happy birthday," she said. "I hope you like your present."

Grannie returned the kiss, eagerly folding the dainty girl in her arms. Esther was a junior teller at the bank, and she was dressed in her neat uniform on her way to work.

"Have to run now." She patted Grannie affectionately and hurried off.

Grannie watched the young girl out of sight, and then slipped back into the past.

She saw herself again as a young girl like Esther, going off to her job as a maid each morning to the big plantation house. It was while she was a maid there that she had met Joseph. Strong, quiet, mild-tempered Joseph, who had loved her and had married her after a short courtship. A wave of nostalgia swept over her as she recalled the simple ceremony at the Methodist chapel, and the voice of the parson as he bade her repeat after him. "I, Selina, do take thee Joseph to be my lawful wedded husband." She and Joseph had repeated their vows earnestly, determined to keep them until death.

Selina and Joseph had been happy, working hard to make a home, and revelling in their parenthood as the babies came along. They wanted to have a little house of their own, so Selina took in washing and kept pigs to help her husband save the necessary money. Just before their sixth child was born, they realized their dream, and bought the house. Selina, although in her eighth month of pregnancy, proudly helped to paint and decorate it, doing all those little things that make a house into a home.

The baby was born in July, and in December, Joseph died. When Selina was called to the hospital to see him for the last, her mind at first refused to accept the fact. She gazed numbly at his young muscular body, shaking her head in disbelief at its unnatural stillness. But Joseph was dead. A bout of influenza had brought on pneumonia, and her children's father had breathed his last. Selina felt she would die too from desolation and grief during those first awful weeks following her bereavement, but she was left with six children to support, she had to go on somehow.

It was no easy task, washing other people's clothes, scrubbing floors, working part-time at the plantation.

Selina kept her large family as best she could, but her small earnings gave them only the bare necessities, and sometimes, more often than not, even less than that.

It was about four years after Joseph's death that the Stewarts moved into the neighbourhood. Marjorie, her eldest child, came home one evening after school. "Mamma, mamma, some old people move into Mr. Grant big house!" This house had been untenanted for some time as the rent was fairly high. "Old people?" Selina questioned.

"Yes. And them is furriners."

"How you know them is furriners?" Selina asked."

"Cause them does talk down-along, nuh!"

Selina did not question the child further, but she wondered what kind of people they were. If they could rent Mr. Grant's house, they must be pretty well off. The next morning she handed Marjorie a bowl of fresh eggs.

"Go and see if the people in the big house want any eggs."

"You mean the furriners?" Marjorie asked.

"Yes, I ain't got a drop a kerosene to put in the lamp tonight so try and sell them, hear?"

Marjorie ran off obediently. When she came back, she had not only sold them all, but was full of news about the foreign lady.

"Ma, she fat, fat, fat, and she got 'bout six bangles pon she hand, real gold bangles!" Selina listened to the child with interest. "And, ma," Marjorie went on, "she ax me 'bout my family, and I tell she my father dead." Then she added after a pause, "she real nice too. She give me cake!"

Selina sent Marjorie the next week to the foreign lady, but she herself never saw anything of her. Then one morning a neighbour called out.

"Selina, I hear the lady in the big house want a washer. Why you don't go and see if you could get the job?"

"Soul, I don't think I could wash another rag when the week come," Selina said, but she badly needed the money, so she went next morning. Going up to the back porch of the big house, she rapped timidly on the door.

"Someone there?" asked a female voice with an unusual accent.

"Yes, ma'am," Selina answered.

Presently the door was opened by the owner of the voice. Selina saw at once that she was not really old, she had only seemed so to Marjorie's childish eyes. But she certainly was fat, and she did wear lots of gold. Gold bracelets, gold rings, gold chains, and even gold teeth.

Selina came straight to the point. "I hear you wants a washer, ma'am."

"Is only me and me husband, so it ain't much to do." The lady spoke in the sing-song tone which immediately proclaimed her to be a 'foreigner', as Marjorie had said; that is to say, a native of a West Indian island other than Barbados. Then she continued in a friendly manner.

"I can't remember seeing you before. You live nearby?"

"Yes, ma'am," Selina answered. "Is my lil girl does come with the eggs."

"Oh! You is that child mother? She nice lil one. But she tell me she father dead."

"Yes." Selina felt a stab of pain at the recollection. The fat lady clicked her tongue in sympathy.

"How you managing with all them lil children?"

"It hard, but I does try my best, ma'am." Selina never complained about her misfortune, but the struggle to raise her six fatherless children was becoming increasingly tough, especially now that they were growing older. She could have put some of them to work on the plantation, but she wanted her children to go to school. So, she took in more and more washing until her weekly load was so heavy, that she lost many a night's sleep in order to finish the ironing.

Mrs. Stewart's washing was not much, but she paid well. In fact, Selina found her a very generous and friendly person indeed. The Stewarts took pleasure in befriending Selina and her large family. Mrs. Stewart was especially taken with the children, and was always sending or bringing some gift to delight them.

For a whole year Selina washed for the Stewarts, and Mrs. Stewart proved to be more like a friend than an employer. Sometimes she would visit Selina and engage her in friendly talk as she worked.

On one such occasion she came panting up to Selina's door with a letter in her hand. "I just hear from home, eh!" she said, waving the letter to-and-fro. "They want me to come back."

"Where you people live, ma'am?"

"You don't know?" Mrs. Stewart was surprised. "I is a St. Lucian bred and born, but me husband is a Bajan."

"And you gwine back?"

"Yes. I going." She looked at Selina for a long time before she spoke again. Then she said almost hesitantly, "I was thinking . . ." She broke off to trace a pattern on her broad lap. "I was thinking I would like to take one of your children with me."

Selina halted in her journey to the glowing coal pot on the doorstep, the iron in her hand.

"Tek one a the children?" She was silent for a moment. "That is very kind of you, ma'am, but . . . I . . . I don't know." She paused again. "Which one you was thinking of?"

"Any one, my dear. Whichever you think best. You know I will take good care of it."

There was no mistaking the sincerity of Mrs. Stewart's offer. It had taken Selina completely by surprise. She just couldn't think of anything to say.

"Look," Mrs. Stewart said, as she rose and made ready to leave, "You think it over and I'll come and talk it over with you another time."

Selina continued her ironing in a 'brown study.' The idea of giving away one of her children repelled her strangely. And yet, wouldn't it be rather selfish to deny one of her children the sort of home the Stewarts could provide? They were, as she had proven, a kindly and religious couple, and they had been more than kind to herself and her children. It would not only be selfish, but ungrateful to say no to Mrs. Stewart's request. After all, she'd still have five left. Maybe she wouldn't miss just one.

So, she reasoned with herself, and had almost settled the matter in her mind when the children began to arrive from school. She ran to open the back gate when she heard the voices of Marjorie and the two youngest, Letty and Joan. "Good evening Ma," they chorused. "

"Evening, children, evening," Selina answered as they entered, and she was immediately reminded of her conversation with Mrs. Stewart. Joan, the youngest, ran up to give her a kiss. This little one had not known her father, and Selina felt a special tenderness for her. She couldn't give away her baby, she thought, as the small arms encircled her neck.

Letty, who was a little older than Joan, was quiet. Quiet like her father. Selina was often reminded of her husband when she looked into the grave eyes of the little girl who was so much like him. She would certainly miss Letty if she gave her away. But then, she told herself, Mrs. Stewart would not be able to manage such young ones.

In a short while, Marjorie called from the kitchen.

"Ma, I gwine wash up the wares 'fo I feed the chickens, hear?" Selina remembered again the understanding and companionship Marjorie had shown after Joseph's death although she was only eight years old at the time. She had sensed the great burden her mother had been called upon to bear, and had rallied like one far beyond her years. In fact,

Marjorie was a companion as well as a daughter. No, she could never part with her.

The boys went to a more distant school, and they came in almost half an hour later. Boy-like, they came bounding into the house, forgetting the formal greeting the girls so easily remembered.

"Who you all speak to?" their mother scolded.

"Evening ma," they shouted. Geoffrey, the eldest, was a tall boy for his age, and was doing so well at school, that his teachers had entered his name as a candidate for a grammar school scholarship. But Selina knew that she would hardly be able to supply the necessary books, should he succeed. Maybe Mrs. Stewart's offer was a golden opportunity to have him educated.

The other two boys were twins, Joseph and Nathaniel, and they shared her husband's name. Mischievous, untidy, loving, and funny, they went everywhere and did everything together. They were beloved by all the family.

Which one? That was the question which revolved in Selina's mind as she sat at the kitchen table with her six children that evening. She reflected how kind it had been of Mrs. Stewart to make such an offer, and how much it would mean to the particular child. Geoffrey was the one who needed the opportunity most. She would be unselfish and let him go and live with the Stewarts for his own sake. She made a firm resolve to give Mrs. Stewart her answer, and almost succeeded in quelling the rebellion in her own heart. The remaining days of the week sped by, filled with the hard, driving, work she had set herself to do. On the following Monday when she went to collect the washing from Mrs. Stewart, she would give her the answer. On Saturday evening she noticed that the children were whispering among themselves and casting furtive glances in her direction, but she was tired and took little notice of them, except asking mildly, "what wrong with the bunch a you all?"

Ah well, tomorrow was Sunday. Tonight offered a brief respite from work. She went to bed early.

She always made a habit of rising as soon as the prison bell rang at five o'clock in the morning. But this Sunday morning she was awakened before the bell sounded. Some noise had roused her, and she lay there wondering what it could have been, and slightly annoyed that some of her rest should have been stolen from her.

And then she was startled a second time by the noise. It came from directly outside her bedroom door.

"Happy birthday to you!" six lusty young voices were singing in unison, though scarcely in harmony.

"Hey!" Selina jumped out of bed. "I forget today was my birthday."

She opened the door and the children bundled in still singing. They placed a parcel on the bed, and Selina's eyes shone with pleasure. She opened the parcel but could not see well enough in the faint light of dawn, so she lit the little kerosene lamp. The parcel contained their gift, a little brooch made of sea shells; and, too, there was a birthday card. Selina fingered the little brooch delightedly.

"But this is too purty!"

"You like it, Ma? We do it we self." The shells were stuck on to a piece of cardboard in the shape of a fish, and at the back a small safety-pin served as a catch. On the birthday card was inscribed in various hands:

To our dear Mother

Marjorie, Geoffrey, Joseph, Nathaniel, Lefty,

JOAN.

Joan, who had only just learnt how to write, had evidently insisted on inscribing her own name, and it sprawled across the card in wobbly capital letters. Selina hardly knew if she wanted to laugh or cry as she tried to embrace her children all at once.

"Wear it, Ma!"

"Pin it on, put it on!"

She obligingly pinned the brooch to her nightdress, and as they all crowded around her, chattering and laughing, the question came back to her mind. Which one should she give to Mrs. Stewart? Which one could she do without? And, more important, which one of them would want to be separated from the others?

After the children had gone, she stood there a long time holding the card in her hand, reading it over and over. Those six names belonged together. Along with herself, they made a family, and they were very happy together in spite of their poverty.

She raised her head and looked through the window at the clear daylight breaking through the mists of dawn. She stroked the quaint little brooch on her bosom and breathed a deep sigh. Her mind was made up. She knew the answer she would give to Mrs. Stewart. Next morning Selina went to collect Mrs. Stewart's washing. The fat lady opened the door herself.

"Morning, child. You make up your mind yet?" But before Selina could reply, Mrs. Stewart had gone back indoors to collect the clothes. When she returned Selina made the little speech she had so carefully rehearsed.

"Mrs. Stewart, ma'am, please don't think me ungrateful, ma'am, but I has come to tell you that I can't give you neither one of my children." She stared down at the floor, expecting Mrs. Stewart to protest; but after a long pause she looked up to see the fat lady gazing at her steadily. "Please, ma'am, don't think me ungrateful . . . " Mrs. Stewart cut her short.

"I understand, chile, I under-stand; and I think you done the right thing." Her voice was warm and kindly. Selina was a little taken aback by the unexpected words; but Mrs. Stewart continued. "Perhaps I was wrong to ask you such a hard question, but I not vexed with you." She laid a large plump hand on Selina's shoulder. "I ain't going forget you. You will hear from me when I go away."

Selina could think of nothing to say, so she remained silent until she had tied up the bundle of soiled clothes and was ready to leave. Then she said with feeling, "The Lord bless you, ma'am."

True to her word, Mrs. Stewart kept up a steady correspondence with Selina, and it was mainly through her interest and assistance that Geoffrey was able to attend the grammar school when he won the scholarship. She was a friend Selina would never forget.

The years rolled by, bringing many changes in Selina's life; years in which the affection of her children amply repaid her for all the early hardships she had endured. And now, as she sat in the old rocking chair on her ninetieth birthday, she fingered tenderly the brooch pinned to her gown, the same brooch which had assisted her in making a vital decision.

She was recalled to the present by the ringing of the postman's bell. Her daughter Joan, with whom she now lived, ran to get the mail and Grannie asked expectantly "Anything for me to-day chile?"

Joan brought her three birthday cards and some parcels. The cards were from Geoffrey, Nathaniel, and Letty. Her children had made a ritual of sending her cards and presents on her birthday, no matter how far away they lived. Joseph's card had arrived the day before from the U.S.A. Joan's card had been tucked under her breakfast plate that morning. There was only one card missing; Marjorie's. Death had again put in its grim appearance when Marjorie had died, still a young woman. "Ah well," Grannie sighed as she opened the first envelope, "The Lord giveth, and the Lord taketh."

Joan, guessing the thought that had given rise to the remark, hastened to cheer her up.

"Come, Ma, look at the presents the grandchildren send!" Grannie brightened immediately.

"Bring them chile. Bring them and open them for me." And the old lady proceeded to examine the contents of the various parcels with as much pleasure as she had experienced on that early morning so long ago.

TWO

FATHER BEAR

A young woman with a baby on her hip and a toddler holding on to her skirt, stepped into the tiny one-door shop. She rapped on the counter and waited. After getting no response she rapped again. This time she was answered by a growling querulous voice.

"Who that out there? You gwine lick down the place?" The young woman dared not answer. She knew from experience that it would be better not to take any notice of his rude question. So she continued to wait, and while she did so, she looked around the little wood-and-coals shop which Mr. Baine had kept for as long as she could remember. It had changed very little since her childhood. It was merely a little more untidy. When Mrs. Baine was alive she had tried to keep things neat, but still there was always coal dust on everything in spite of her labours. It lay thick everywhere; on the counter, on the floor, on the scales, and even on the glass jar with the sugar-cakes which Mrs. Baine made and sold to children. But now she had been dead these seven years, and the shop missed her care. The young woman heard his heavy tread as Mr. Baine came into the shop from his back-yard, and she felt the old thrill of fear as he looked at her.

"What you want?" he growled. Mr. Baine growled like a bear and he looked like one.

"A ... a ... bundle ah wood," she stammered. Somehow she couldn't help being afraid of the man, although she was no longer a child but a married woman with two children of her own. Mr. Baine was a big man, though not fat, and quite black; so black that the young woman as a child had thought that he'd been blackened by the coal-dust. He had bristling and bushy eye-brows with a moustache to match, and a fringe of grey hair hung over his collar escaping the old felt hat which he always wore. Very thick spectacles rested on a bulbous nose and his few remaining front teeth leered menacingly when he spoke. This combination of features made him appear almost inhumane, and he always reminded her of Father Bear in the fairy tale.

Interrupting her reflections, Mr. Baine placed her bundle of wallaba sticks on the counter, and, as he did this, the baby on her hip leaned forward and pulled at his moustache. "No!" She pulled back the child with a little gasp, but to her surprise Mr. Baine smiled. Feeling some confusion, she hastily gathered up the wood and prepared to leave, forgetting to hand over the money.

"Hey! A penny fah that!" Mr. Baine roared. Whereupon she almost flung the penny on the counter and went out. The young woman lived but a few yards away from the shop, so she soon reached her home. Passing through the back gate with the children, she stopped short as a sound came from the house. She'd left no one there but it was easy to guess who was inside. With a slight sigh and a new drag to her feet she went into the house.

"Pearl, that is you?" It was her husband.

"Yes," she answered. Victor came out of the bedroom.

"Where you went?" Then seeing the wood, he said, "Oh, you went at Mr. Baine shop!"

"Yes, Victor . . . ?" A question was upon her lips but somehow, she began to talk of Mr. Baine instead. "That man always remind me of Father Bear in the story."

"What man?" Victor asked.

"I mean Mr. Baine. You know when the bear say 'Someone has been tasting my soup'?' Here Pearl imitated Mr. Baine's growl. Victor laughed and she laughed; too loudly and a little too long. The children, looking surprised at first, joined in the laughter too. Then there was a sudden silence.

The baby said "Da Da!" and held out her arms to Victor. He took her, and Pearl began to get busy with the coal pot. Then she could hold back the question no longer, though she was afraid of the answer she would get.

"Victor, you get . . . get . . . "

"No!" Victor answered before she could finish. Pearl turned to the task of lighting the coal pot again, and this took care. First, she had chopped some of the wood into slender sticks; then she'd placed a bit of rag soaked in kerosene in the centre of the coal pot with the sticks around it. Now all she had to do was strike the match. She did this, but the match dropped and went out. Her hands were shaking a little. She lit another and this time set the coal pot ablaze. Placing the pot on the fire, she sat at the kitchen table and began to prepare their lunch. Green bananas, sweet potatoes, and a handful of bonavista beans picked from a vine in the yard. That was all. The vegetables were soon peeled and put into the pot with a little salt. Then Pearl lifted her eyes and looked at her husband, and he winced at the despair he saw in them.

"Victor, what we gwine do?" she asked. "The man say he gwine put we out a the house if. . . if. . . " Her eyes filled with tears and she could not go on.

"Don' mind he, girl. He can't very well do that," Victor tried to cheer her up, speaking with a confidence he was far from feeling. He had been a soldier, and had come through many a difficult situation during the war, but this poverty, this unemployment, was threatening to overwhelm him and his young family. He dropped his head onto his folded arms. Pearl looking at him, spoke.

"We could sleep at Aunt Bee, but she house too small to hold we things. What we could do with them, Victor?"

"I tell you the man can't put we out so," Victor assured her. But Pearl felt doubtful. She couldn't believe, as her husband did, that the man wouldn't do such a thing. He had looked really grim the day before when he heard once again that they had no money to pay.

"Look, this t'ing can't go on no longer. You got to get out ah my house by tomorrow evening or I gwine put you out," he'd said. He had given them many chances before, in spite of similar threats, but Pearl felt sure that he meant to do as he said this time. Her mind was sick with worry over their plight, but irrelevantly, she began to talk about Mr. Baine again.

"You know what happen today, Victor? Baby pull Mr. Baine moustache, and he laugh . . . Victor you hear what I say?"

"Eh? . . . Oh, who laugh?"

"Mr. Baine. Baby pull his moustache."

"Huy!" Victor answered with little interest. Then he got up abruptly and headed for the door.

"Where you gwine?" Pearl asked him.

"Oh, . . . anywhere," he answered carelessly.

"Victor try an' tink up something befo' tonight," Pearl pleaded. "Don't let that man put we out."

"Don't worry, baby, I gwine do something." He went out promising to come back for his dinner.

After he had gone, Pearl cried a little; softly, to herself, wiping away the tears with her sleeve. When she and Victor had got married, she never imagined that life could become so difficult for them. To be sure, she had seen poverty all around her in the village as a child. Her own parents were not too well off but somehow they'd always managed to feed their children and keep a shelter over their heads. Her mind reached back into the years when she was a little girl. Almost everyone in the village had been poor. She and the other children had gone to school barefoot and had gone in droves to the stand-pipe for water, as at that time, running water in the home was a luxury. They shopped daily for their mothers at the small shop which served the village with essential groceries such as rice, peas, salt-fish and cooking-oil. Mostly they prefaced their shopping with the speech "Ma tell you to send . . . " because they were asking for credit, and the shopkeeper would mark the amounts in his well-thumbed note book.

Pearl remembered, though, that Mr. Baine never gave credit. If anyone hadn't the necessary cent or penny to buy his wood and coals, he had to borrow or go without. A hard man, who seemed to desire the company of no one. Since his wife's death, his sole companion was a mangy black cat; and Pearl had seen him smile only once before today. She remembered the incident clearly.

As usual, she and some other children had gone to his shop together. It was a hot day and Mr. Baine was perspiring and uncomfortable. Adding to his discomfort was a persistent fly trying to alight on his nose. For about the fourth time Mr. Baine gave a violent swipe with his hand in an effort to get rid of the pest; and this time he knocked the glasses from his nose.

Mr. Baine was very short-sighted, and the children laughed as he felt about the counter for the glasses, missing them narrowly many times. But Pearl did not laugh. The sight of Mr. Baine without his glasses was most strange. She was surprised to see how helpless he looked. A blind Father Bear. Somehow his pathetic fumbling about the counter did not amuse her, so she picked up the glasses and put them into his hands. Then she moved away quickly, for Mr. Baine was a ferocious bear again the moment he put on his glasses.

"Who dat pick up my glasses?" he growled. Pearl trembled.

"Is Pearl," the children said.

"Who Pearl?"

"She!" They pushed her forward. " Is she, Mr. Baine." Pearl stood silent, feeling naked under his fierce regard.

"You is Pearl?"

"Yes," she whispered. Mr. Baine turned, and without a word, took one of the sugar cakes from the jar and gave to her. Pearl was too surprised to say her thanks at first; besides, she was occupied with the children crowding around to share her prize. After a while she cast a shy glance in his direction and he smiled. Just a slight lifting of the corners of his mouth, but 'Father Bear' had smiled! Since then Mr. Baine had never taken any more notice of her, and she had certainly not seen him smile again until today when her baby had pulled his moustache. That had been the only bright moment in this depressing day. She sighed again as she realized their sad condition and felt even more depressed as the day advanced. Supposing they were really put out? How horrible! How shameful it would be! And what could they do? Pearl struggled against a rising panic within her as she did her chores. Victor was not even there to reassure her. He had not come back for his dinner as he'd promised. It was getting on to six o'clock when she heard the knock.

"Who that?" She asked in a frightened voice.

"Come open this door! Who that what?" a rough voice answered. Her heart jumped at the words and the tone, and she went to the door.

"You want me?" she asked.

"Mr. Pollard send we to put you out ah he house." There were two other men standing by, silent and unconcerned. Pearl said and did nothing for a while. Then she spoke.

"All right," and stepped into the road with the two children. Was this really happening? Or was it a nightmare? She stood in a sort of dream and watched their few possessions being thrown roughly by the roadside. She didn't even cry; just watched. In a short while a crowd began to gather to witness their shame; but Pearl hardly noticed them. Where was Victor? Pearl began to wonder about her husband. If only he were there. Why hadn't he returned as he'd promised? Then, as if in answer to her thoughts, Victor came pushing through the crowd. He came straight to her.

"Pearl! Pearl! What happen? Stop! Stop! I get a job this evening." He turned to the men who were coming out of the house. They had finished their job. "Wait! Wait a minute! I get a job. I going settle with Mr. Pollard tomorrow."

He tried to argue with them, but they brushed him aside. "Move, man!" The man in charge closed the front door and locked it. By this time the crowd, ever growing, had become noisy, and the baby in Pearl's arms began to cry. She was so occupied with hushing the child, that she never noticed his arrival until she heard his growl close to her.

"Where wunna going put these things?" It was Mr. Baine. But Pearl could not answer. She could only shake her head; but Father Bear understood. He looked at her intently for a moment, and Pearl saw something in his face that she had never seen there before. He touched her baby with his rough hand. "Poor lil soul," he said. Then he turned to Victor and pointed to the scattered pieces of furniture in the street. "Come, put you' hand and help me here," he said.

"What? What?" Victor seemed unable to understand.

"Looka, man, we ain't got all night. The rain set up. Come along!" Mr. Baine commanded, and Pearl and Victor, assisted by some of the lookers-on, carried out his instructions.

It was only when they had managed to put everything inside Mr. Baine's rather stuffy house, that Pearl could reflect on what had happened. It had all been a horrible dream until Mr. Baine had come. Why had he come? Why had he done what he'd done? She couldn't find any answer, so she set about with a thankful heart, though still in a daze, to settle into her new surroundings. The next morning Pearl still found herself at a loss for words. She wanted to thank Mr. Baine, to tell him how deeply she and Victor appreciated all he had done for them, but Mr. Baine was his grouchy self again. He was bending over something in the kitchen. He looked up, saw her, and scowled so ferociously that she didn't know how to begin.

"Morning, Mr. Baine," she ventured.

"M'ning," he growled.

"Mr. Baine, Victor and me would like . . . "

"All right, all right." He brushed her aside and walked into the shop.

"You is still a old bear," Pearl said to his retreating back, and turned to the preparation of breakfast with a perplexed frown. After thanking Mr. Baine and receiving a similar growl, Victor had gone off to his new job early, leaving Pearl and the children in their new-found shelter. A little later in the day, Pearl missed the two children, and went all through the house looking for them in vain. Then an awful thought struck her . . . suppose . . . suppose Mr. Baine, the old bear had . . . had . . . but, no, that was too terrible a thing to contemplate; and then she heard a distant childish giggle. It came from the shop. She ran to the door breathlessly and stood still at what she saw. Mr. Baine was sitting with the children on his knees, smiling into their upturned faces. Pearl drew a little closer. His familiar growl reached her ears. He was telling them a story.

"Then the three bears come back to the house and the big big bear say . . . " Pearl stopped to listen to his recital of the old story of the *Three Bears,* a happy smile on her face.

"Father Bear," she whispered, "Dear Father Bear!" She would never be afraid of him again.

THREE

THE SHOE

When I first saw the shoe, I hardly noticed it. It was barely discernible in the half-light of 'fo'day' morning. I had been sent to fetch the milk as usual, and, as I came 'round by the side of the house, shivering in spite of the protection afforded by one of my father's old jackets, I saw it on the ground, just below our front window; but I did not give it more than a glance. What was holding my attention was the alternating advance and retreat of the sea on the shore on the other side of the road. Living right next door to the sea as I did, this should have been an ordinary spectacle to me, but since the hurricane, I had come to regard it with something of awe.

Now as I ran along, from time to time, I would cast a glance of morbid fascination at the white crests of the waves, and wonder when I would see them billowing and hurling themselves across the road as they had done on that day not so very long ago. I had other things to occupy my mind too. This morning I would be back at school again as the Easter vacation was now over.

Mr. Drayton, the man who sold the milk, lived some distance down the road, so that it was quite light when I returned with my mother's pint. As soon as our house came into view, I noticed with amazement a small crowd gathered in front of it. I could see them gesticulating, but could not hear what they were saying. I hurried on, and, just as I reached the house, I heard my mother's voice above the hubbub.

"Clemmie, don't touch that shoe!" (Clemmie was my father.)

"How you mean don't touch it?" he queried, straightening up from his examination of what proved to be the shoe I had observed on my way out.

"Don’t you touch it!" Ma insisted. Her voice sounded hysterical.

"But this is all foolishness," my father said. "What you expect could happen if I touch the shoe? Woman, don't be stupid." But, still, he did not touch it.

By this time, I had come closer and so I had a good look at the shoe which was the centre of attraction. It certainly was a strange-looking object. As one woman in the crowd aptly put it: "I never see a shoe like that in all my born days. What kind a foot could get into that thing?"

"And the sock," another exclaimed. "Blood red!"

"Woman, why you don't hush you mout'? You never see neither red sock yet?” This from a youngster in the crowd. The woman pounced on him.

"What you know 'bout it? You just born yesterday and you gwine tell me 'bout these things? I tell you, that isn't no ordinary sock. Look at all them marks 'pon it!"

Everyone drew nearer to look, including the scoffing young man. The thing really looked sinister. The shoe, I believe, was once tan in colour, but now it had a patchy whitish-yellow appearance, and it had the strangest shape I had ever seen on a shoe. The toe swung to the left and the heel to the right, and it was so 'spraddled' in the middle that it was difficult to tell at a glance whether it was a left or right foot shoe. It carried no laces, and the eyelet holes gaped like hollow staring eyes. A brilliant red sock hung over one side half-in, half-out of the shoe, and it was spotted with small blackish marks of different shapes and sizes.

Still, ugly as the shoe and the sock were, I wondered why such ordinary things should cause such consternation. However, I soon found out as I listened to the talk going on all around me.

"Nellie," a woman was saying to my mother, "Tek it from me, the body that put that shoe there ain't got no good mind for you. You best had try to get it off a yuh premises. " Ma stood staring at the shoe with a frightened expression, and the woman came closer and placed a hand on her shoulder as she continued to enlighten my mother. "You see that red sock? It mean blood." She paused dramatically. "And that twist-up shoe is to show that somebody gwine twist up in pain."

Ma burst into tears. "O dear, o dear, I ain't do that woman nutten." I looked at her startled. What woman was she talking about?

Then someone said "How you mean you ain't do that woman nutten! You think Babsie is a fool?"

The woman who said this was a long-time enemy of my mother; she and my mother were always quarrelling. As for Babsie, she was my father's wife. They had separated some years now, but they had grown-up children. My mother and Babsie, of course, were not on speaking terms, so now they were blaming Babsie for this horrible shoe, which somehow suggested obeah to everybody.

When I looked at my mother again, the same woman was speaking to her, but now in a whisper, and my mother was nodding her head vigorously. By this time it was growing late, and, as they were all working-people, the little crowd soon dispersed, and my parents and I went into the house.

There was a strained silence in our small kitchen as we had our breakfast. My father said nothing until he had put on his hat and was ready to go out of the door with his bag of tools. Then he turned and said to Ma "Nellie, you know very well that Babsie ain't had nothing to do with that old shoe. Why you let that woman tell you so much foolishness?"

"I ain't want to hear nothing 'bout Babsie. All I want to tell you is this — don't carry my child at she again." She shook a warning finger at my father, who went through the door in a huff.

My father had often taken me to visit his wife although they had ceased to live together for many years. She was much older than my mother, and I believe she was older than Daddy too, but I really liked Aunt Babs, as I called her. She lived all alone in her little house since both of her children had gone away. She always welcomed me, and gave me nice things like corn pone and coconut bread. If I happened to go on Saturday, there would be pudding and souse.

Now there was quite a lot of talk in our village about obeah, and the things I had heard sometimes kept me awake at night. But Aunt Babs had always scoffed at such talk. "I puts my trust in the Lord," she would say. I didn't know whether the presence of the shoe under our window had anything to do with obeah, but I was quite sure that Aunt Babs had had nothing to do with it; so I was determined to go and tell her about the incident, despite what my mother had said. That afternoon I left school as soon as I could, and ran through the gully, taking the short cut to her house. I burst through the gate panting.

"Chile, what happen? What happen?" Aunt Babs was in the kitchen cooking, and I had startled her.

"Aunt Babs . . . " I began.

"Sit down and ketch yuh breath first chile, then you can tell me what happen." And she pushed me into a chair. "Here! Drink this water." I gulped down a little water and then told her all that had happened that morning.

She clapped her hand to her breasts when I told her that they all thought she was working obeah for us. "No. Not me. I had nothing to do with the works of the devil," she said solemnly in denial. Then she continued, "But why your mother think I want to do she something?"

"I don't know," I replied, for I was just as puzzled as she was.

"All that happen between me and she happen long ago. The Lord knows I don't bear hatred in my heart for she or your father."

She turned back to her pot. "All that obeah talk is foolish talk. Don't believe in that nonsense. Don't let it confuse you chile."

After I had had some of the sea-egg soup she was cooking, I told her goodbye and ran home, feeling much more certain that all that talk of obeah was indeed foolishness.

My mother did not suspect that I had gone anywhere after school, and I said nothing to her, but I longed to tell her that Aunt Babs wished her no harm, nor had done her any harm. I was certain that the shoe was merely a shoe and nothing else, although I did not go near it, and I was still a bit frightened when I went to bed.

I had been sleeping for what seemed to me to be a long time, when I was awakened by the sound of voices. I listened for some time, then crawled out of bed and peeped through the window.

The moon was shining brightly. What I saw fascinated me. Ma and the woman who had talked to her that morning, and a strange man were outside. The man wore a long bright chain around his neck, and he was pouring something out of a bottle on the shoe. It was his voice I had heard. He was chanting some strange words in a monotonous voice, words that I could not understand. Ma and the woman stood with their backs to him, so still that they looked like statues in the moonlight.

When the ceremony was over, the man raked the shoe and the sock on to a flat piece of tin, and the three of them, holding it between them, walked toward the sea.

I watched them until they were out of sight, and then closed the window and got back into bed. It was a long time before I dropped off to sleep. I kept seeing the flash of the long bright chain in the moonlight, and heard again the drone of the man's voice, and I shivered with horror. Suppose there was such a thing as obeah, after all.

I was only ten years old at the time, and although I was deeply impressed by the incident, my childish mind was soon occupied with other things.

Yet I could not put the thought of what had happened that morning wholly out of my mind. A shadow seemed to have been cast over our home. Daddy seldom joked and laughed now as he used to, and Ma complained of headaches and became very fretful; and very often they would quarrel over mere trifles. I, too, often felt lonely and unhappy during that period, as time passed, and eventually the school term ended.

The long summer vacation had begun, when one morning as I was running along the pasture at the back of the village. A boy's voice called out to me: "Noreen! Noreen!" I looked back.

"Hello Tony," I replied. "You spending the holidays down here again this time?"

"Yes." He was eager to talk to me. He was a big boy for his age, but he wasn't very intelligent. In fact, we all considered him rather stupid. He could hardly read, and he couldn't speak very clearly. I wanted to move on. "You c-c-c-could tum and play with me?" he mumbled.

"Not now," I answered, "my mother send me to the shop," I certainly didn't want to play with Tony.

"S-s-stop a minute, though," he went on. "Y'know when I was here at Easter I lost one of my shoes . . . I take off one . . ."

I didn't wait to hear his mumbled jumbled account of how he had lost his shoe. I was looking down at his feet. They had the queerest shape, deformed almost. I did not wait to hear any more. Leaving him staring after me, I ran home as fast as I could. Ma was ironing clothes.

"You come back from the shop already?" she asked, but I paid no heed to her question. "Ma, Ma," I spluttered. "I find out 'bout that shoe. It belong to Tony, the half-foolish boy that spend the Easter holidays at Miss Payne up on the hill. Is his shoe. He lost it."

"What . . . who . . . what?"

"He out 'pon the pasture now. Go and ax him." I rushed off not heeding the volley of questions that Ma poured at me, and ran off, down through the gully to tell Aunt Babs. She was right after all. All that obeah talk was just foolishness.

Daddy and Ma wouldn't be quarrelling anymore now. I felt so happy.

FOUR

RED LETTER DAY

The day began like any other in Maxine's orderly life. She'd risen from her bed the moment the familiar march had started on her Rediffusion speaker. Sylvan, her husband, slept on peacefully, snoring a little. The sky through the open window showed dark blue. It was going to be a fine day and Maxine felt at peace as she sang along with the choir, the hymn that marked the beginning of the early service on Rediffusion. It was no time to start the breakfast yet, so Maxine went into the yard and began to sweep. As usual she could hear old Ma Connell next door doing the same thing.

"Morning ma," she sang out.

"Morning chile," Ma replied.

"How yuh this morning?' It was a kind of ritual and Maxine knew just what she would hear.

"I ain't well at all chile. These two eyes ain't close for the night. The pains in the two ole knees nearly kill muh"

"Cuh-dear" Maxine sympathized.

"But God say who he love he chastise." Ma Connell consoled herself.

Maxine made a suitable answer and soon returned to the kitchen. By this time Sylvan was awake and dressed. He and his wife conversed in the unselfconscious manner of people who spend much time together and feel at ease in each other's company.

"Yuh find de white fowl yet?" Sylvan asked.

"No bo. De tiefing people won' leh she go."

His question reminded her that she hadn't fed the fowls and she fetched the tin of shelled corn and went to the door calling "chick cum chick chick chick, chick cum."

"This is 'bout six fowls duh tief from you this year," Sylvan said between noisy sips of coffee.

"Yes," Maxine agreed, three when Miss Jones had the excursion, two at Easter and now one more. I don't know how much more I gun loss before Christmas.

"Why yuh doan put them up?"

"Steupse! Dah is more trouble than profit Duh cahn tief all."

The Rediffusion announcer's voice came clearly through the kitchen during a lull in the conversation. "The time is exactly three and a half minutes to 8'o' clock."

"Hey wuh leh me get outta dis place bo. I ain't know it did so late. Sylvan jumped out of the chair wiping his mouth with the back of his hand. Soon he had got out his bicycle and was on his way. Maxine watched him fondly as he rode out of sight; but a small sigh escaped her as she went back into the house. Her's was a happy marriage; there was no doubt about it. Sylvan was a considerate husband and a good provider; but after all these years, they still had no children.

"Well," Maxine said to herself, ashamed of her discontented feelings. "You can't have everything in this world." She pushed the thought to the back of her mind and set about to do her housework. Sylvan would be home by 12.15 for lunch so she finished as soon as possible and prepared to go to market to shop for the meal. The moment she came out of her door, she saw the bus passing in the main road and broke into a run, shouting "who ooo! who ooo!" The conductor kept the bus until she got there.

As Maxine climbed into the bus panting and perspiring, a voice hailed her from behind. "Hey Maxine girl, wuh I ain't see yuh fah long enuff."

Maxine turned around and recognised the girl who spoke to her. "Gloria what you doing down here?"

"I going down at my aunt in Gibbs Road. How yuh keeping?"

"I all right for de time being. How de children?" Maxine asked.

"Duh well." I ah . . . " Just then the bus gave a lurch as it narrowly avoided hitting a cyclist. After the slight commotion Gloria continued. "I does see yuh husband up by me sometimes you know."

"Up by you?" Maxine looked puzzled.

"When he come to look fah de chile. Yuh know de girl nus-ed to live up that way?"

Maxine stared at Gloria in shock surprise, unable to say anything.

"You din know?" Gloria asked.

Then Maxine noticed the curious glances of the other passengers and said in a hurry, "Oh yes, but I forget." And turned her back on Gloria.

There was a curious cold feeing in her stomach as Maxine stared straight ahead hardly noticing anything around her. She heard Gloria's voice echoing over and over in her mind. 'What girl? It couldn't be true. wasn't true.' Though she tried to reassure herself, the icy fingers still gripped her middle. Somehow, she managed to say goodbye to Gloria quite naturally as she got off the bus. Her shopping done, she returned in good time to prepare the lunch. As she moved about the kitchen her thoughts went around in circles.

'He been deceiving me all this time and I ain't know a word 'bout it. Wait till he come home,' Maxine promised herself viciously. Then the tears began to fall into the salad she was mixing. "He doan want me nuh more cause I can't give he no children," she sniffed in self-pity. That was what hurt Maxine most of all. Her beloved Sylvan not only had another woman, but had had a child by her, while she herself, his wife, could not give him one.

She and Sylvan had waited patiently at first, confident that they would have a baby before long. But when three years had gone by and Maxine showed no sign, she had secretly visited a doctor to seek help. The doctor had been optimistic and assured her that he saw no reason why she could not have children. He had given her a prescription and told her not to worry, but now after eleven years of marriage, she was still childless.

However, Maxine had found a recent outlet for her frustrated motherhood. A retired nurse had started a day nursery for babies of working mothers in the neighbourhood. She had appealed for help and Maxine had volunteered to give four hours, three times a week. She really enjoyed herself now working among the babies, washing nappies and preparing bottles. Sometimes when she cuddled the warm heads against her plump bosom, she felt like a mother.

Little Rickey was her favourite. He was just 18 months old and had been coming to the nursery for the last 6 weeks. His mother had gone to the United Kingdom leaving him with his grandmother who worked as a domestic, so the child was brought to the nursery every morning. Maxine felt a great pity for the little boy, for she knew he would be missing his mother; and recently she'd gone to the clinic more often just to be with Rickey.

She had been anticipating with pleasure her stint of duty this afternoon but now she could think of nothing but Sylvan's infidelity and deception. As 12 o' clock drew near, a little of her anger subsided as she hurried about the kitchen, putting the last touches to the meal and setting the table. By the time Sylvan rang his bicycle bell and Maxine went to the door, she had almost forgotten the incident. When he came inside though and kissed her, memory flooded her brain and she felt so confused and embarrassed that she found herself at a loss for words. She decided to leave the matter until he'd had his lunch but she had no appetite herself and pretended to be busy.

"Eat your food woman." Sylvan said noticing that she had not been eating. At the sound of his voice, anger boiled up in Maxine again.

"I ain't eating at the same table wid you, yuh old deceiver."

Sylvan dropped his fork and looked up in amazement. "Wha wrong wid you now?" He tried to sound nonchalant but his pulse had raised in alarm. 'Oh Lord,' he thought, 'she find out.' He knew that Maxine did not fly into a temper at nothing and he was sure the secret he'd kept for so long was out at last; but he still pretended not to know what Maxine was talking about.

"How I deceive you?"

"You ain't know how you deceive me? All this long time you got another woman and coming to me talking 'bout love. You even got a chile from she. You think you could fool me all the time?" Maxine was in fine metal now as she stood before Sylvan, with her hands on her hip and her eyes blazing."

"Who malicious body tell you that now?"

"So you ain't deny it. Yuh ain't even shame. You think I cuh live wid you now?" There was a break in Maxine's voice. "I know that you don't want me now cause . . . cause . . . " The tears poured down her face and she collapsed on to a chair, face in hands. Sylvan jumped up in distress and went to Maxine.

"Maxine don't cry nuh, don't cry. Stop crying nuh! You is my wife and I love yuh," he pleaded.

"Don't talk to me 'bout love."

"You mean you would brek up we marriage because of one foolish girl?"

"How she foolish and yuh is still guh to she every week? "Maxine looked at him accusingly.

"I got to gi de chile something." Sylvan opened his mouth to explain further but he had touched on a sore point, the child that was not hers. Maxine broke into fresh tears and ran off to the bedroom, slamming the door.

Sylvan left half of his lunch on the table and went unhappily back to work wheeling his bicycle down the rocky gap staring unseeing before him, his thoughts in a whirl. Doreen, the girl who was his child's mother had been only a passing fantasy with him and he'd taken pains not to let the affair come to his wife's knowledge. But then she'd become pregnant, and although he could not help being pleased, after all this would be his first child, he felt dismayed at the thought of his wife finding out about it. He had not liked keeping the child a secret from Maxine, but a man couldn't go to his wife and say, 'Well darling my girlfriend had a baby yesterday, it's a boy.' So he had said nothing about it but paid short visits to the child every week to carry his allowance and to enjoy his clandestine fatherhood.

Every time he came away he thought to himself. 'This should be our child, mine and Maxine. If only Maxine would have it.' But he thought that would be too much to ask of his wife. Besides he was afraid of how she would take it.

Meanwhile Maxine was crying her heart out at home. She felt that life had ended for her; but when the storm of hurt and anger had spent itself, her brain felt washed and cleared by the tears. After a while she began to think in a calmer frame of mind. 'What is the use of me crying?' she asked herself. 'What done done and nutten can't undo it.' She began to wonder now about the child. Was it a boy or was it a girl? She thought of Sylvan holding it and felt intense jealousy of the woman who had given him such pleasure. A foolish girl, he'd called her. Did he really think so little of the child's mother? Suddenly Maxine wanted to find out all she could about this child, Sylvan's child; but she did not like to go snooping around. She couldn't have people laughing at her for a jealous wife. She dried her tears and went about the house briskly, washing up the dishes and tidying. She remembered that this was her afternoon at the nursery and the thought of seeing Rickey lifted her spirits a little. Arriving in good time Maxine greeted the paid nurse and other helpers pleasantly.

"Good evening everybody."

"Good evening Miss Bowen," the nurse replied, then asked, "You looking for Rickey nuh? For Maxine had been looking in all directions and everyone at the nursery knew how she loved Rickey.

"Yes. Where he is. I ain't see he nowhere," Maxine said.

"Maxine you ain't hear 'bout Rickey?" one of the girls asked.

"Hear what?" Maxine sat down suddenly feeling weak in the knees as she sensed disaster.

"Wha happen?"

"The grandmother bring he here this morning in a state," the girl said. "It seem she had the day home and she was cooking some cou cou and the child get scald with the okra water."

"Lord havist mercy! He dead?" Maxine asked in alarm.

"No he ain't dead but he burn bad. She bring he here first thing aas it happen but nurse tell she to carry he to the hospital."

"How long it happen?" Maxine asked.

"'Bout 10 o' clock this morning. The grandmother bring back a visiting ticket just now. You could see he this evening."

Maxine sat staring before her pensively. This was a black day for her. First the news about Sylvan and now Rickey. Poor little Rickey, she sighed. Of course she would visit him often.

Now that this had happened, Maxine realised how strong her feelings were for the child. It was as if he were her own. She went about her duties for the evening with a desolate air, watching the clock anxiously till it was time for her to leave. She meant to go straight to the hospital. It crossed her mind fleetingly that she knew none of the child's relatives except the grandmother; but that did not deter her. She had a right to see Rickey. Hadn't she tended and loved him like a mother for the last six weeks?

As usual, there was a crowd outside the hospital gate battling with the orderlies who were letting in the people one by one.

"Stop pushing," an orderly shouted. Maxine recognised the voice. It was a fellow she'd known as a boy.

"Sonny, leh me get in," Maxine called, edging through the crowd.

"Hey Maxine honey how you? Who you got in here?"

"A lil boy. I don't even know if he dead."

"He's you child?"

"I ain't got nuh children; but leh me get in fast."

"All right, all right, all right." He let her in and Maxine went up to the children's ward. She went straight to Rickey's bed hardly noticing the man who was standing there looking at the little boy.

"Rickey," she called softly but the child was sleeping and did not answer."

"Maxine, what you doing in here?" Maxine jumped and for the first time looked at the man beside her.

"Sylvan! Sylvan but . . . but . . . "

"Maxine, this is the lil boy." Sylvan said.

"Wha lil boy? You mean . . . you mean . . . ?"

"Yes, he is my child."

"But this is little Rickey," she said foolishly.

"Right," Sylvan said with an air of satisfaction.

She stood looking silently from Rickey to Sylvan, her mind trying to grasp the facts. Now that she saw them together, she could see the resemblance. So this was the child. A child she'd already learned to love. Breaking the silence, Sylvan said with a note of pleading in his voice, "the mother gone to England and leff he. Maxine we could . . . we could . . . we could." He looked searchingly into his wife's face. Maxine was silent for a long time then she answered his half-spoken question with a broad smile. Sylvan sighed with relief and put his arm around his wife. They stood together gazing fondly at Rickey until a voice behind them said,

"Lady I am sure you 'd be able to take home yuh little boy next week. He get off very light."

"Oh yes mum. Oh thank you mum. Maxine beamed upon the nurse. 'Her little boy.' she'd said.

Maxine was happy. Wonderfully happy.

FIVE

THE BLUE BLUE SEA.

The large black bellied sheep heavy with young, bleated as the girl came up the grassy slope towards it. She'd come to take it home; but first the girl kept straight on to the edge of the cliff and stood there quietly looking out to sea. She did this every evening when she came to collect the sheep.

Janice was just an ordinary 16-year-old girl, not pretty, just pleasant to look at. She did all the things a country girl of her age and station did, but she had this one eccentricity, this peculiarity; she loved to look at the sea in the twilight. It turned such a pretty dark blue then and looked so mysterious in the fading light that she felt a weird fascination as the waves boiled and slapped on the steep shore, bursting over the boulders and flinging spray high into the air. Janice usually stood for about 20 minutes on the cliff until the night closed in 'round her; then she would run for the sheep which would be bleeding piteously by this time, going home at a swift trot.

But this evening, soon after she came to the edge, she noticed that she was not alone. A young man stood only a few yards from her, a dark silhouette on the bare cliff. Had he seen her? He gave no such indication as he turned his head and looked in her direction; but not at her. Then Janice started. "Is Robin," she said, under her breath. "Robin, that St Lucia boy." Why wouldn't he look at her? He must see her standing there. But Robin took no notice. She so wanted him to speak to her. The sheep began a steady bleating but it hardly penetrated her consciousness.

Robin was the most talked of boy in the neighbourhood. When he had first come to work on the plantation, all the girls had been crazy about him, but Robin didn't seem to care. He remained aloof, working long hours for Mr Drayton at the plantation house, though no one seemed to know exactly what work he did. The chauffeur at the big house said that Robin did anything from gardening to bookkeeping. Now here he was on the cliff looking at the sea, just as she was. This opportunity to speak to him was too good and she couldn't miss it. She edged quietly along the cliff until she was quite near to him but still he seemed not to see her.

"Hello," she said.

"Uh huh." Still he did not look. At least he must have seen her since he had grunted an answer to her greeting.

"The sea look pretty this time of evening." No answer. "I mean it does get blue blue." Robin looked straight out to sea ignoring Janice completely and she began to feel offended. If this stuck up boy felt he was too good to speak to her, he could drown himself in the sea for all she cared. His handsome profile however, could not be ignored, and she couldn't help noticing how smooth his dark skin was or how proudly he held his head. From the looks of him, this boy was worth knowing. She tried again. "I does come up here every evening." This time he looked at her and spoke.

"Yes, I does see you with the sheep sometimes." His accent was foreign but Janice expected that, she'd heard that he had come to Barbados with the cane cutting gangs.

"Ohh." She was thrilled to think he had noticed her. "I like to watch the sea. You too?"

"Yes, I like to watch it."

"Where you come from the sea pretty like this?"

"No, it ain't half so pretty, but then, it's all the same when done, all water."

"Yes, I know that, but . . . "

"You can swim?" he interrupted.

"No. You?"

"No, I cannot swim. That is a good thing though."

"A good thing? How you mean?"

Robin did not answer. He'd gone silent again, staring at the turbulent water and wrapped in his own thoughts. The sheep bleated again and Janice began to move, but slowly.

"I got to go home now."

"What you name?" he broke in suddenly.

"Janice." She was delighted that he'd asked. "Janice Payne. I know your name already though."

"Yes, everybody know my name 'bout here. They does talk 'bout me. You hear anything 'bout me?"

"Like what?" Janice was puzzled at his question.

"You don't hear nothing 'bout me?" he pressed.

"Well!" In fact, she had heard things about him. People said things about him and the white girl, the master's daughter, but Janice didn't like to say that. "Well, all the girls say you's a cool cat," she said. Robin was certainly a good looking young man.

"Oh?" He looked at the water churning beneath them. At the point where they stood, the sea came rushing under the cliff, eddying and whirling angrily. It was the most dangerous part of the coast.

"Anybody does bade here?" he asked suddenly. She'd heard, but the sudden change of subject surprised her. Wasn't he pleased to know that the girls liked him?

"No no no! You ain't see how de water getting on? Nobody would be so foolish as to bade here. They would get drown."

"Yes, I see." He was silent for a while, staring down at the water, and Janice became a little uncomfortable. Then Robin looked at her, really looked, as if he'd only just seen her. "Janice." His voice was soft. "You got a boyfriend?" This was better, but she hesitated before answering.

"Yes." She hadn't, really, unless you could call a boy who always said something nice to you a boyfriend, but it seemed as though Robin expected her to say yes.

"Yes. You got a girlfriend?"

"I . . . I . . . I don't know." His voice sank to a whisper and his face hardened, making him seem even more handsome than before.

"I . . . I love a girl but I can't say she is my girlfriend."

"And the girl love you?" Janice asked.

"Yes, I think so." He paused then. "You in love with this boy?"

She giggled. "hmm. Not so much, we does only talk." Robin did not answer. The night was closing in swiftly around them and the sheep broke the silence with its plaintive bleating. Janice started. She'd have to go now; it was time to take the sheep home.

I going home now Robin but I gun, . . . I gun come up here tomorrow evening." There was an invitation to her voice but Robin took no notice.

"The water turning black now," he murmured. "Black black as night."

"Yeah, but I like it blue. Deep blue, just like now."

"Blue or black, all is the same."

Janice began to move off. Robin frightened her with the way he spoke. He suddenly turned away from his contemplation of the water and came close to her.

"Go home Janice. Go carry in the sheep." She felt a tingle of excitement at his nearness, but the strange expression in his face gave her a queer feeling. What was this boy thinking? What did he have on his mind? Janice reached out a hand to him in spontaneous sympathy; then, Robin held her and kissed her full on the lips. She was startled but pleased. "Go home Janice," he murmured, giving her a little push, and Janice went. She was glowing inside as she pulled up the stake and started down the slope with the sheep.

She went slowly, but kept looking back at the boy. Even when she stepped on to the highway, she could still see him through the shrubs. Then, she stopped suddenly, rooted to the spot, for she saw Robin's figure disappear. He'd fallen into the sea; and couldn't swim. He'd said so. He'd said something else too; that it was a good thing he couldn't. He hadn't fallen at all, he . . . he. Janice screamed as her thoughts came to the horrible conclusion. Leaving the sheep to make its way home, she ran straight to the plantation house where Robin worked. The chauffeur turning into the driveway, stopped the car suddenly to avoid running her over. As soon as Janice saw him, she broke into incoherent speech.

"He jump in the sea! He jump in the sea! He jump in the sea! Come quick!"

"Wait wait wait wait! What wrong? Who jump in the sea?"

A young white girl who'd been sitting in the car got out. "What's wrong?" she asked.

"Robin," Janice answered. "He mussee drown by now."

"Robin jump . . . ?" The chauffeur stopped suddenly for the young girl at his side had slipped quietly to the ground in a faint.

"Oh Lord looka trouble. Help muh here girl! Miss Annie gone and faint straight away. Janice stared in open mouthed surprise for a moment before she responded to the chauffeur's call for help. Then something clicked in her mind. Why had Miss Annie fainted when she heard about Robin? She thought about the afternoon just gone and a light dawned upon her.

"It true then. It true." Janice had spoken aloud and the chauffeur looked at her.

"Uhh?"

She said nothing else. She couldn't talk about it. Instead she asked, "Wha 'bout Robin?"

"Wha 'bout he? If he chose to drown heself in the sea I can't help that." Janice knew that the chauffeur did not care for Robin, and she hated him.

Mr. Drayton was shocked by the news when he heard it, but by then there was nothing he could do. Robin would now certainly be dead.

The body was never found and Robin was soon forgotten in the village; but Janice long remembered his handsome face as she saw it in the twilight on that evening. She remembered too the strange kiss he'd planted on her lips. She wondered too, if that other girl remembered, the girl he'd loved.

A few days later, as Janice went for the sheep, she saw a figure on the cliff. It was that of a girl, slim, with long hair streaming in the wind. The girl stood still, gazing out to the sea, just as Robin had done. Janice watched the still form for a long time then sad and sick at heart, she turned and went home. She hadn't looked at the sea in the twilight since that tragic evening. The blue blue sea had lost its charm for her

SIX

THIS LAND IS MINE

"Reuben! Come! Yuh food ready! Reuben!"

"Ah coming now!" Reuben answered from the yard. His wife came to the back door and stood watching him for a while. She had called him three times already. She studied his bowed head and the stooping dejected shoulders, shook her head and called.

"Ain't no use bothering yuh head now Reuben. Ever what happen, happen for the best."

"I coming now Girlie," Reuben repeated but he didn't move. 'Everything for the best,' Girlie always said that. No matter what happened, it happened for the best; but he couldn't believe that, for tomorrow he and his family would be leaving their home. He and his family had to pack up and leave. He'd been dismantling his wooden house to put it up elsewhere, leaving the trees that he'd nurtured and the land that he had cultivated and loved.

"Reuben!"

"All right All right." Reuben turned abruptly and entered the house. It was supper time and he and Girlie sat at the familiar table.

"Where de boys?" he asked.

"They ain't come home from school yet. There got a football match this evening so they watching it."

Thinking of his two sons, reminded him of his cousin and himself when they were boys. They'd grown up together like brothers. He, Reuben, had had no parents. His mother had died when he was a baby and his father had never taken any real interest in him. His cousin Roy's father, uncle Doug, his mother's brother, was the only father he'd known. Roy was uncle Doug's son, but it was Reuben who accompanied old Douglas Thomas on donkey cart trips to the market with the produce of his little farm. He and his uncle would work side by side helping the hired men cut and load their few tons of cane. He'd learned from his uncle all there was to know about planting and husbandry. Roy was a little older than himself and was a very bright scholar, and the old man was naturally proud of him; but Reuben was the old man's right hand in the running of the small peasant farm. It was Reuben who kept him company and whom he depended on to keep things going smoothly. Inevitably, there had grown between uncle and nephew a companionship which sprung from interests shared. Roy saw this and became jealous. Reuben was aware of his cousin's antipathy but he chose to ignore it. That jealous heart, was now after all these years, taking its revenge.

Finishing his supper during which time he had hardly spoken another word, Reuben rose and walked out of the house, across the yard and up the steep slope that lay beyond. At the top of the little hill he stood looking out to the Atlantic, a dreamy look in his eyes. It was here on this ridge that he and uncle Doug had talked that far off day. Waving a sinewy arm, the old man had said, "Ben boy there's nothing like a piece of land to make a man a real man. It belong to you and you belong to it. And when yuh got it, you and yours gun never hungry." He had paused for a moment, casting a loving glance over his crops of sugarcane and vegetables, then he'd continued.

"I real please to see how you tek to de land boy. My boy Roy is a bright boy and I well proud of he, but you got the birth-right Ben." A thrill had passed through Reuben when the old man had said that, for he had often wondered if his uncle would consider leaving any of his property to him. He knew that he had no right to expect it, but the land had gotten into his blood just as it had into his uncle's. Reuben kicked a pebble and watched as it rolled down the grassy patch to the strip of rocky terrain that separated their land from the sea. And, echoing over the years he heard uncle Doug clear his throat and speak those words, the words he had wanted to hear most of all.

"I thinking of building a new house over there," indicating a flat space to the right of where they were standing." The house for Roy; but I gun leave my old house and this piece a land over here for you boy. I know you would make the most of it." Overjoyed, Reuben had thanked his uncle. He knew then how much he wanted to stay on that bit of earth and already he felt the pride of ownership. The swift darkness coming now over the sea recalled him to reality. He walked back slowly to the house. Girlie met him with a snort of impatience.

"But where you been all this time? All the work in this place to do and you out there with yuh hand in yuh pocket staring out to the sea? This ain't nuh time for moping and moping. Yuh getting on just like yuh lost yuh mudda. Man, yuh mek muh shame." She flounced off.

Reuben took her scolding in silence. It was true he was moping when there was work to be done. Along with the two boys, who by this time had returned, he set about doing the heavy jobs entailed in moving. Tomorrow would soon be here.

Uncle Doug had told Roy of his intention concerning Reuben. Reuben knew that his uncle had meant what he said that day on the ridge but the old man had never made a will. He had trusted Roy to carry out his wishes. Then one morning he and Reuben were working in the field. One moment he was sticking his fork into the earth, the next, he had fallen senseless before his nephew's shocked eyes. They had carried him into the house and the doctor had been called but uncle Doug had never opened his eyes again, nor had any word passed his twisted lips after that.

Reuben felt such a sense of loss at first that he never thought of the property until he was forced to. By this time both he and Roy had married. Roy had done exceedingly well at school, now held a good position in the civil service and motored to work every day from the new house on the highway. Reuben and his wife occupied the old man's house and he looked after the land.

With his uncle dead, he had long since realised that he'd owned nothing but he still relied on his cousin to honour his father's wishes. He prospered, in a moderate way. As time went on he added to the old house and bought a small car. He lived a contented life with his wife and their two sons. He took it for granted that things would continue as they'd always done. Someday, he and Roy would talk the matter over and the necessary papers would be drawn up. Roy seemed to be a good fellow. He had all he wanted.

Then one afternoon, Roy brought a stranger to see him, an Englishman. Reuben wondered at the reason for this unexpected visit, for Roy was not in the habit of calling on him often. They sat and chatted for some time on a variety of matters. Finally, the conversation turned to tourism and it was then that Roy revealed himself.

"Ben," he said "ah Mr. Chelston here has offered to buy the land at a very good price."

"De land?" Reuben repeated. For a moment he couldn't understand what his cousin was talking about.

"What land?"

"My land. This bit of land. He wants to develop it into a hotel and a holiday resort. Man, I think it's a great idea." Reuben sat mute and unbelieving.

'My land,' Roy had said, not 'our land.' Why, he had not even consulted him about the sale. Reuben could think of nothing worse than to have all this beautiful arable land converted into a building site. It would be a sinful waste. As from a distance, he heard Roy's voice continuing and saying to him. "You and I will talk about it later Ben man . . . hmm." He and the visitor rose to their feet and bade him goodbye.

After they had left, Reuben sat in the same position as though he had been stunned. When Girlie, who had been busy with her various chores in the yard entered, she noticed his distraught appearance and enquired what had happened. But he would give no answer and continued to stare into space. 'My land,' he thought. Gone! Sold! Sold to a stranger. Me and my wife and children ousted from my home. 'This land is mine,' he thought rebelliously. 'The land belong to me. It is mine, mine, mine.' But he knew he could lay no legal claim to it, and there lay the rub. Roy returned in due course for his talk with Reuben, but there was really nothing to discuss. The property belonged to Roy and he was selling it, that was that. He would allow Reuben to keep the chattel house on condition that he moved it off the land. He could keep it "for old time's sake," Roy had said; but Reuben had made no reply.

The months went by and Reuben and his family now moved to a small plot of land about half a mile away and tried as best they could to pick up the threads of their old life in new surroundings, but Reuben felt hemmed in. There was little room on his new holding for expansion; and then one day, Girlie said to him

"Ben, yuh see yuh don't have nutten much to do pon this land. Why you don't tek the car and work it?"

"Work it? How? Wha it ain't a lorry. And even if I sell it, de money wun be enough to buy a lorry. Wha you mean work it?"

"Listen to me Ben. You been noticing lately how many tourises does come up here to look round? Now I know you loves this land; but you can't work it if yuh ain't got none; so I did thinking you could work wid de tourises. You knows up here good good good. They would be glad fah somebody like you to show dem round. Wha 'bout that Ben?"

Reuben looked at her attentively. The woman had an idea. There was logic in what she said. After some discussion, Reuben decided he would give the matter a trial. He procured the necessary license and set out for Bridgetown in a new spirit of adventure.

Now that he was actually in this new business, he lost some of his hurt. It took some time for him to get properly started but soon he was making regular trips to hotels and beauty spots all over the island. He began to see his country through the eyes of his customers and his mind, always sensitive to beauty, revelled in the serenity of the countryside. Best of all was when he brought visitors to his own native hill and showed them the sites he'd always loved. They usually caught his enthusiasm and enjoyed their tour all the more for it. But yet when he looked down on the old familiar homestead as yet unspoiled by the proposed project, he felt again the sharp pangs of exile. However, he prospered in his new venture and found a measure of contentment.

A parching hot August brought in its train as usual, a very wet September. Reuben and his wife lay in bed one night unable to sleep, listening to the rain pounding on the roof. Suddenly they heard a slow rumbling noise followed by loud crackling sounds and heavy thuds.

Girlie jumped up.

"Wha happen! Wha dat! Wha dat?"

"Must be thunder," Reuben replied.

"Dah ain't nuh thunder, Girlie said."

"Something like it fall down. Must be de cow pen."

They switched on the yard light and peered through the driving rain; but everything appeared to be in order as far as they could see, so they went back to bed.

By 5.30 the rain had stopped and Reuben rose to a sodden wet morning. "Nah business fah me today," he thought. As he looked out on the forlorn scene, he saw a little group of labourers coming down the road. They were talking loudly and excitedly.

"Mr. Thomas! Mr. Thomas!" one of them shouted. "Come and see what happen. All yuh cousin land gone clean in the sea. Evah bit gone!"

"What you mean?"

"All yuh cousin land slip and gone in the sea last night. He house fall down."

"But Roy! Roy all right?"

"Yes Mr. Thomas. Dem all get out in time but is a terrible thing to see yuh." The speaker winced at the memory of what he had just witnessed.

"Girlie. Roy land slip and gone in the sea. Come!"

Together they raced up the hill, the two boys ahead of them, for they'd been awakened by the labourers' loud voices.

What a spectacle met their astonished gaze. It was unbelievable and shocking to see the huge colour-crowned banyan tree that had so long lorded it at the top of the hill leaning tipsily on its side at the foot of the incline.

A whole field of young canes had slipped into the sea. Vegetable crops, shrubs and small trees, made chaos at the foot of the slope; but the most astounding sight was the hillside itself. Somehow the landslide had dug long furrows all down its side as if giant claws had scratched deep into the clay surface. Reuben shuddered almost feeling those vicious claws on his own flesh. Dazed and stricken, he gazed on the scene of destruction. He had always thought of land as something enduring, something that could not be destroyed; and now, this. The land that had been the mainstay of his life and of uncle Doug's, all torn to pieces and tumbled in an untidy heap and so much of its precious soil washed away forever.

It was a long time before any of them spoke. Girlie was the first to break the silence.

"Wha looka God work. You see now that unfair never prosper?"

SEVEN

THE WEDDING

Marilyn woke suddenly to find the sunlight streaming across her bed. At first she couldn't think why she felt so excited, but it came to her in a moment. Tomorrow was to be her wedding day. Her wedding day. It seemed almost too good to be true. Would everything be all right? She had an uncomfortable little feeling that something might go wrong but she put the thought from her mind. Yesterday the girls had given a shower for her. She worked in the lingerie department of a clothing store and her workmates had presented her with a negligee, all decorated with five and one dollar bills. It was all lovely. The gifts, the congratulations, the posing for photographs, everything. Getting married, Marilyn thought, was the best thing that could ever happen to a girl; and getting married to George, was just perfect. Marilyn had met George when they were both at school. That was years ago; but they'd fallen in love only recently. It was as if they were seeing each other for the first time then. However, they were going to be married, and tomorrow she and George would walk happily down the aisle, a radiant and handsome couple. Yet, that thought wouldn't leave her.

"Lynn?" Marilyn jerked out of her dream world as her mother's plaintive voice penetrated her thoughts.

"Yes Mama I'm coming."

"Chile yuh got to go to the hair dresser this morning. Why yuh don't get up and get ready?"

The voice came nearer as her mother poked her head in at the bedroom door.

"All right all right." Marilyn was already dressing, when she asked, "Mama, Van finished the cakes yet?"

"Every long time since," her mother answered. Yuh aunt phone to tell me they come since yesterday evening."

"Oh, I want to see them. I hope they pretty."

"Duh got to be. I paying enough." Mrs. Foster started back for the kitchen. "Come and get something to eat girl."

Marilyn finished her breakfast and hurried off to keep her appointment with the hairdresser. Leaving there, she stopped at her aunt's to see the cakes. The reception was to be held at Aunt Vie's home, and when Marilyn arrived, her aunt was in the bedroom looking at gift parcels, so she had a good look at the cakes all by herself. There were four in all, two made in the shape of horseshoes and trimmed in green and gold, a round one decorated with pink flowers, and the magnificent bridal cake, four tiers high, with the bride and groom at the top. There were also ducks and a cleverly contrived pond on the second tier. Aunt Vie came up behind her.

"You like them Lynn? "Personally, I think Van do a splendid job."

"Oh yes," Marilyn agreed; and she hugged her aunt in a sudden overflow of emotion. "Oh Aunty everything is so wonderful."

"Hope it would be always so." Aunt Vie hardly shared her enthusiasm. Maybe she had a premonition, for in a few moments, a chain of events started which almost ruined Marilyn's wedding day. There was a knock at the door and Aunt Vie went to answer.

"Hey Miss Carter, come in, come right in." Mrs. Carter came in, trailed by two small children of about four and five years respectively.

"Hello Vie." The two women exchanged kisses; then Aunt Vie took notice of the children.

"Come and kiss auntie," she said and they both complied. "May, you just come in time to see the bride, she's here now."

"Oh, I brought a little gift for her."

"Come inside the bedroom then." Aunt Vie took the gift and piloted Mrs. Carter into the bedroom, leaving the children outside admiring the cakes. Marilyn sat on the bed with Aunt Vie and Mrs. Carter, chatting pleasantly, woman talk. That made Marilyn feel admitted into the marriage circle already. They must have talked for a good twenty minutes before Mrs. Carter rose to go.

"The wedding is half past four," Aunt Vie was saying as they passed the drawing room. "We looking for . . . oahhh!" she stopped suddenly with a gasp of dismay for Mrs. Carter's two cherub children stood before the ruined bridal cake looking guilty.

"Stop that! Stop you little wretches!"

"Oh Auntie," Marilyn cried in horror while Mrs. Carter ran to her children.

"Dennis! Jean!" she shouted. Jean began to cry, her tears mingling with the bits of icing on her chin, while she wiped her eyes with a fist full of sugar roses. Dennis looked contrite, but went on devouring a headless duck which he held in one hand while he wiped the sticky fingers of the other in his trousers. Aunt Vie collapsed onto a chair with a moan.

"Twenty-five dollars. Oh, twenty-five of the best dollars that that cake cost and now these lil pigs come and spoil everything."

"Vie I sorry that this happened but you don't have to call my children pigs. After all they's only children." Mrs. Carter sounded hurt.

"Children!" Aunt Vie flung back angrily. "Any children who would do that they is pigs I say. And furthermore, the person who got them to train ain't nuh better."

"Oh dear," Marilyn thought. "I knew something bad was going to happen." She tried to intervene. "Aunt Vie don't say that, we can fix back the cake." She turned to Mrs Carter. "Don't mind what she say. She's only a little upset."

But Mrs. Carter felt insulted, and holding her children's hands, she marched stiffly through the door with a terse "Come!"

The cake was repaired at a little extra cost. Mrs Carter did not appear at the wedding, and she was estranged from the family for a very long time after that.

Marilyn's wedding day began fine and sunny. Which meant according to popular belief that she and George would live happily together. But still that uncomfortable nagging feeling persisted. Would anything happen to spoil the wedding day? Three o' clock found her at her dressmakers from where she was to leave for the church and at twenty minutes to four, the lovely white bridal gown was thrown over her head for the first time, since she'd followed an old custom, never to try on the bride's dress beforehand. Marilyn viewed herself in the mirror with a gasp of pleasure at the lovely picture she made.

"Oh my!" the dress maker beamed. "I know you would make a pretty bride. Come Grace, come and see." Grace, her assistant, came in and obligingly admired Marilyn. Then the dressmaker set about zipping up the fastening at the back but the zip wouldn't budge beyond the waist.

"But what wrong with this thing nuh?" she complained.

"See if it catch something," Marilyn suggested anxiously.

But that was not the trouble. After much running up and down of the zip, the dressmaker had to admit wearily, "The waist too small. You mussee put on weight since I measure you."

It was now five minutes to four and Marilyn's father would be coming at 4:10 to pick her up. Oh, she knew things would have gone wrong. The dress was pulled over her head in a hurry and Grace began to unpick some of the seams while the dress maker measured her afresh. "A whole inch more," she sighed. "You been eating too much Miss Marilyn."

"It will take long?" Marilyn questioned, watching the repairs.

"No, not so long; but yuh father gun have to wait."

"Oh dear," Marilyn wailed. "And I promise George not to be late." But late she was. In fact, almost half an hour late and when she reached the altar on her father's arm, she sent George a quick apologetic glance as the minister hastily started the service. When the congregation began to sing the well-known wedding hymn, Marilyn forgot all the previous mishaps and thrilled to the lovely singing. This was her day. There she stood before the altar, radiant and happy and beautiful in her lacy white gown as only a bride can be. She looked up at George and caught him gazing at her, and he smiled as she lowered her eyelids modestly. George, she thought, was the handsomest bridegroom that ever stood before an altar. Marilyn didn't think of George for long however, for as the organist started on the last stanza of the hymn, a raucous voice rang out loudly, almost drowning the other voices. Marilyn jumped.

'Oh no,' she thought, 'not today. Oh Uncle Jim, how could you?' In fact, her uncle Jim had come to his niece's wedding tipsy and was now indulging in drunken antics. Marilyn consoled herself with the thought that the hymn would soon end; but uncle Jim had other plans. As the voices of the congregation ended in a diminuendo, he started briskly again, marking time with a fist on the back of a pew. Marilyn just stood there and suffered. Oh everything was going wrong on her one wedding day. Would he never stop? She ventured a glance at George and he winked ever so slightly, which was his way of saying that he understood how she felt but that it wasn't so bad after all. Then growing tired of his own solo, uncle Jim stopped abruptly and the ceremony continued without further mishap.

The drive to her aunt's, let it be said, was uneventful, but Marilyn had now become nervous, expecting something to go wrong at every turn. But nothing happened and it was with a feeling of relief that she stepped out of the car and entered the house. Congratulations and kisses were showered upon George and herself as they stood side-by-side. Then the imp that was dogging her all day poked its head out again as her uncle Jim came to give her an embrace. For uncle Jim flowing with affection, embraced and kissed, kissed and embraced, tighter and tighter and louder and louder. Marilyn gasped for breath, pleading in a weak voice "Oh Uncle please; oh Uncle!" before she was rescued by George who firmly unwound Uncle Jim's arms from her limp body. Marilyn felt awful. She was certain her make-up was ruined by all those wet kisses, and what a fool she must look. Everything was going wrong. She looked at George to find him actually smiling. Marilyn felt cross now with him. How could he smile? However, George, straightened her veil and gave her hand a little squeeze, all of which made her feel considerably better.

In a short while, Marilyn changed to a sleek blue dress, coming out to find the guests relaxed and enjoying themselves. Uncle Jim of course managed to do a little more than that, but no one minded him.

The wedding reception went smoothly until the time came for making speeches. The master of ceremonies was her cousin Phillip from the civil service. Toast after toast was proposed and drunk with much cheering and laughing at witty sayings. Then George's uncle rose to speak. He was a small country farmer and his accent and speech was as rustic as himself.

"Ladies and gentlemen." He was saying now. "I have one piece of advice for the bride groom tonight." He paused for effect then continued. "Yuh goin hear people say that these is modern days and things is changing. I ain't deny that; but leh me tell yuh ah lil secret." Here he held his ear. "Womens don't never change. No sur! From Adam day down to this, they is woe to a man, and they need to be keep in order. So what I say is this, don't leh she wear the pants man. Be a man in yuh house, even if yuh got to nuse yuh stick. There was a moment of shocked silence after he said this; but before he could add anything else, Uncle Jim banged his hand on the table angrily.

"Hey you! What you mean by that? You telling he to beat my niece?"

"I ain't say so," the man defended himself, but uncle Jim wasn't listening.

"Yuh best know yuh place. My niece too good fah that poor tail boy she married this evening. If he lay sommuch as a finger 'pon she, he gun get to answer to me. So he best doan play de fool hear?"

"Order! Order!" Phillip shouted in an effort to stop the row but the two uncles seemed to be enjoying themselves.

"He ain't good enough for you niece you say. Wha leh me tell you something. That boy cuh-da married a high-class lady if he like but . . . "

"Order! Order!" Phillip sounded so stern that the two men stopped abruptly. He called on someone else to speak and then everything went as planned.

Marilyn felt sick and ashamed at what had occurred. Uncles it seemed, were the worst relatives to have. George nudged her and she looked woefully into his face. "Don't let those two old fools bother you sweetheart," he said. Marilyn stood thinking for a moment. Maybe they were just that, two old fools, and not worth bothering about. George was right of course. By and by, it was time for them to get into their car and go. Marilyn sat holding her husband's hand, while the chauffeur got behind the wheel.

"Whew! What a day," George said.

"What a day," Marilyn repeated mournfully. Everything had gone wrong and now George was all upset too. That premonition had been right, her wedding day had been spoilt.

She felt so sorry for George. She glanced at him, but George was starting to smile, then he began to chuckle and suddenly, Marilyn wanted to laugh too. Now that it was all over, the unusual events of her wedding day seemed extremely funny. She began to giggle light heartedly. Then they both bursts into such joyous shouts of laughter that the chauffeur looked around in surprise before he started the motor.

"Crazy!" he muttered. You got to be crazy just to get married anyhow. Just plain crazy." But Marilyn and George were happy. Just plain happy.

ABOUT THE AUTHOR

Dorothy Lovell (nee Porte) was born in Carrington's Village, an area just off Bridgetown in the parish of St. Michael in Barbados.

She was educated at Carrington's Primary and St. Giles Girls School, having reached 7th standard, and she later took private lessons.

Dorothy's artistic talent surfaced as a little girl when she taught herself to play the piano at her modest home in Gittens Road, Government Hill; and as a seventeen-year-old, provided the musical accompaniment for the congregation at the Gittens Gap Mission church. Dorothy married John Lovell in 1951 and she became his deputy organist at the Belmont Methodist church not far from their home in My Lord's Hill.

Her skill as a writer came out in the short stories she penned as a housewife, married and raising five children; and as a youth leader who mentored many a young person. She also became a central figure in the writing and production of plays for performances put on by the Women's League of her church.

Dorothy's five children, eleven grandchildren and three great-grandchildren still live in Barbados.

Dialect Words	English Translation or Explanation
ain't	is not; are not
'bout	about
Brek-up	break up
chick cum	mouth noise made to call chickens
chile	child
cuh	could
cuh-dear	what a pity
cuh-da	could have
dah	that
dah is more trouble than profit	that is not worth it
de	the
de tiefing people	thieves (people who steal)
de white fowl	the white hen or cock
dem	them
doan	don't
din	didn't
duh	they
duh cahn tief all	they can't steal all
enuff	enough
first thing aas it happen	as soon as it happened
fore-day	first light of dawn
furriners	foreigners
got to gi de chile something	must give the child something
gun	will (verb); am/is/are going to
gwine	going (I gwine – I am going to …)
he doan want me nuh more cause	he no longer wants me because …
hey wuh leh me get outta dis place bo	let me leave urgently
how yuh keeping?"	how are you?
I ain't know	I don't know
I all right for de time being	I'm all right for the time being

ketch yuh breath	catch your breath
kind ah	sort of
leh me get in	let me get in
lil boy	little boy
lil pigs	little pigs
Lord havist mercy	Lord have mercy
mout	mouth
mussee	maybe; perhaps; probably
nutten	nothing
nuh	no? not so?
nuse	use
nus-ed to live	used to live
ole	old
pon. pon it	on; place upon
sommuch	so much
spraddled	sprawled out
steupse!	a sucking noise of disgust
tek	take
these two eyes aint close	I haven't slept
tief	thief
tourises	tourists
wid	with
won'	won't
wuh I ain't see yuh fah long enuff	why, I haven't seen you for quite some time
wunna	you. all of you
you din know?	didn't you know?
Yuh	you

References

Allsopp, Richard. *Dictionary of Caribbean English Usage.* Edited by Richard Allsopp. Kingston, Jamaica : UWI Press, 2003

Barbados Pocket Guide : Bajan Dialect. Sungroup Inc., 2015 https://www.barbadospocketguide.com/our-island-barbados/about-barbados/bajan-dialect.html

"Father Bear." IN *BIM Magazine.* Bridgetown : BIM. Vol. XIII. pp. 25 - 30.

"Granny's Birthday." IN *BIM Magazine.* Bridgetown : BIM. Vol. XII : 45. pp. 167 -174

Perspectives : a Course in Narrative Comprehension and Composition for Caribbean Secondary Schools. ed. Cecil Gray. Cheltenham, UK : Thomas Nelson and Sons Ltd., 1982. pp.41 – 45

"The Shoe." IN *BIM Magazine.* Bridgetown : BIM. Vol. XII : 45. pp. 239.

Printed in Poland
by Amazon Fulfillment
Poland Sp. z o.o., Wrocław

54854855R00049